During Her Last Bath

A Short Story

P.R. Miguel

TRIGGER WARNING

The content of this short story navigates the feelings of grief, and describes in minor details aspects of human death. That being said the content might not be suited for all audiences, please read with caution, your mental health is very important. If this book causes distress of any kind please put it down. Thank you.

DEDICATION

To those who struggle with grief, know that everyone's
journey is different.

One

Serena lies so peacefully in the center of her hospital bed. Who knew our youngest sister would be the first to pass away? We certainly did not see it coming. Her room is decorated in yellow tulips, her favorite flower, alongside lots and lots of angel's breath. She used to say that the smell of roses reminded her of death and funerals, ironic, isn't it, that now tulips will be associated with the same thing in my brain. Our Father, Mother, and three other sisters litter the room in various stages of grief.

Our Dad stands full of anger, blaming everyone in this poor hospital. Cursing and blatantly disrespecting everyone, he throws his anger towards the staff and threatens to sue the living hell out of everyone. But how could we have known she had stage four cancer if she didn't tell us? Serena was within her rights of privacy, and to keep that information from us. But Dad couldn't accept that our little princess would have such an undeserving ending. She was of age to make her decisions, although barely; she had just turned twenty-two and had graduated from college only two years ago.

Mom is sitting at Serena's side, holding her hand and running her hand through her head, effectively combing her hair off her forehead, to put her pale and dusky face in full display. Mom hasn't cried, and that deeply worries me. She tries to hold herself strong for the rest of us, but we worry about her when she does that. Her eyes will be forever haunted by the image in front of us.

Mady, Evelyn, and Rita sit on the couch holding each other as they ride the wave of denial. I cried with them too for a little while, but I had to get up to help the nurses with some paperwork. Dad was too angry and didn't know anything administrative about Serena, and he was especially not fond of the fact that she is a willing organ donor. The nurses gave us a while to sit in here, and wait for the rest of the family to come say their goodbyes. Serena looked presentable, but I really wanted to take a moment to give her one more bath, which would have to wait until after our aunts, uncles, and cousins come by. Grandma would stay at home; she had an aversion to seeing or being near dead people.

It's truly unbelievable how quickly everything happened. It was a span of a month when I noticed Serena acting weird. She was always calm and extremely selfless. She gave her heart to everything she did. Not only did I consider her an angel on Earth, but she was our angel on Earth. She insisted on spending time with us, and to some degree, some of us kept brushing her off. How wrong we were to think that time was promised. She taught us a valuable lesson today. She didn't even want to come to the hospital, but our parents persisted, and once she fell unconscious, they brought her here themselves.

The hospital isn't far from home at all. Just a few blocks away, in fact. That was the hospital we frequented when we needed to pay emergency visits, usually for a really bad stomach ache, or some form of chest pain or respiratory reason. On my way to Serena's room, room 5241, in tower two of the hospital. The hallways were getting longer and narrower, with every step forward I took with my remaining sisters behind me. The blood-pumping organ thudded hard in my chest, and my lungs did not expand enough for the amount of air I needed in that moment. We thought she was okay. We thought it was nothing major. We thought we had time. Oh, how wrong we were.

Two

Family filters through the room, taking turns to see her. The lobby is filled with us, and although I am quite embarrassed by all the commotion we are causing, I can't say I'm sorry at all. She deserves to be seen by those who cared, and although, arguably, some of these family members didn't care about her in my book, in their own unique way, maybe they did. And, who am I to deprive them of saying goodbye? Uncles and aunts go in and out of the room. I note that our closest cousins, her siblings, and her two closest friends cried the hardest.

Some of them begged her to come back. Some asked why she didn't say anything. Some wished they could have spent more time with her during her last moments in this fleeting lifetime. I could not agree more with them. As I felt the same way, so many emotions sprouted in my chest as I rode the roller coaster called the stages of grief.

I dared to glare at the family that was taking away the precious time I had left with her, to still feel some semblance of warmth in her limbs and a slight tinge of color in her rapidly diminishing complexion. "Hypocrites." I thought.

I hated them all. But did I? Not really, I just hated that they wouldn't give us a moment to grieve with her. Yes, I know that's really selfish in retrospect, but I don't care. I lost my sister.

She was our everything. The glue that held us together. The flowers that decorated our empty table. The warmth in our household. The space she took in our hearts was immense, and the void would be nearly impossible to fill. And, I would likely die trying to fill that void, as I will be trying to keep her spot on the table open in case her beautiful spirit ever wants to visit us during supper. I will always make sure she has a spot at the table, and I will always make sure she will not be forgotten.

My parents were very religious, and I was more of a skeptic with the belief that there was a higher power. "Evil." I thought.

Whatever that higher power is, it must be evil...Is all that rung in my mind. How could it take my sister?

How could it do that to me? I would have more easily pardoned an amputated leg from my own body. But Serena's life…Never.

It didn't matter; I kept going back and forth between sentiments. My head does not make up its mind. I do not comprehend how she deserved this ending.

As I look at the flowers in the room, my mind flashes back to a moment where Serena and the rest of us were having a picnic. We spoke of grim topics and discussed the afterlife and our very different beliefs. She was more of a religious person compared to me. It was a dusky day, with the sun setting in shades of pinks and very deep oranges. We lay on a thin blanket with two different books, and when she grabbed a flower and twirled it with her finger, her mind wandered, and she spoke.

"You know how we pick the prettiest flowers?" She had said.

"Yeah, so…" I had responded, slightly annoyed that she interrupted me while I was reading.

"I bet God does the same thing." She said.

Irony or pure coincidence? I will never know if she already knew her time was limited then. I would give my own life just to hear her voice again. Damn it! I want everyone to leave already. How am I supposed to cry with all these people here. And, they still wait for her for her honor walk. Apparently it is a tradition among the staff for people who are organ donors.

I approached the nurse and made a simple request.

"Hi hun, what can I do for you?" She said. Her nurse was truly a saint, she brought our whole family snacks and a cart full of snacks, coffee, and water.

"My mother, siblings and I would like to perform Serena's last bed bath. I will ensure to follow any specifications you may have."

"Of course honey. Your sister does not have any lines in her, we took her IV out a while ago. You may bathe her, and please leave her in only a gown. We will take over from there. Is one hour enough?" She asked.

"One hour will never be enough—"

"I'm so sorry hun, I would love nothing else than to give you and your lovely family all the time that you need. But, unfortunately there are hospital protocols and procedures I am vowed to followed."

I sigh. "I understand. One hour starting the moment everyone leaves, please?"

"One hour starting the moment everyone else leaves." She nods in agreement.

Three

Finally, they left. Most of our family went to the waiting area while we bathed her and readied her for her Honor walk. Only Dad, Mom, and our sisters were in the room with her.

"I petitioned the nurse to allow us the honor of giving Serena her last bath."

"Why would you do that?" Mady shot straight up to her feet.

"Why wouldn't you want to help? You'll be okay with strangers giving her last send off into a coffin in who knows what mortuary?"

"You could have asked us," Evelyn says.

"You two can sit out if you want. Raven, Mom, and I will do it." Rita said, as indignant as I felt.

Although I did feel slightly bad for not asking them. I know not everyone would be okay with taking care of or even touching a dead person. But she wasn't just any dead person; she was our sister. Our little sister. Our Serena. Dad would not partake in the bath; he wouldn't be able to handle it. While we prepared the warm water, I received all of the necessary items from the nurse.

Dad knelt by the hospital bed and held her hand in such praise and admiration. As if he were trying to capture the feeling of her skin in his hands. He traced her face with his eyes, and the tears that rolled off his cheeks onto his beard blew up my heart in one million tiny pieces. I didn't just lose my sister. Dad and Mom lost their daughter.

He looked, and looked, and looked. Praying to God that this was all a dream and that she would open her eyes at any moment. He lays his head on her chest and listens to the deafening silence that lingers there. He takes one breaking breath and falls apart on top of his baby's heart, the heart that would soon go to another, maybe...We watched, holding each other as Mom rested her hand on his shoulders, holding together what little energy he had left. One last searing kiss on her cool cheek, and he forced himself to walk out for us to give her one last proper bath with the hands of those who truly love her. Because even after her death, love will not become past tense.

We stood there, trying to figure out where to start. I briefly remembered some classes in care giving I took a few years back. I always thought those skills would come in handy once my parents were old and one of us had to take care of them.

"We should start with her head and face, and work our way down. We can take turns washing her." I said.

They all nodded. And we gave Mom the honor of starting with her hair.

Four

The four of us watched as Mom combed through Serena's hair. At first with her fingers and then with a comb. She has long, luscious brown hair; clearly, she never had any cancer treatment. But why? Did she not feel like fighting? Or did fighting feel futile to her? Maybe she didn't have a choice.

We set an absorbent towel under her shoulder and gave mom the bucket of warm water. She poured the water over her head, and with that, she began to talk.

"You guys might not remember, because you were all little. You four never liked it when anyone touched your hair. But Serena was the oddball. When she was little, she used to bring he comb in the middle of the night so that I could brush her hair to sleep. She loved it when I played with her hair."

"I do remember." Rita wears a faraway smile, lost in nostalgia, "she used to come to my bed too, she would ask me to braid her hair, and once I did." She giggles in between a sob, "She would go mess it up just so that I could re-braid it."

We all watched Mom suds up her hair in shampoo and rinse, and once done, Rita went over and braided Serena's gorgeous hair.

"I was always jealous of her hair; you and Dad only blessed me with like three strands of hair," Evelyn said. "I will miss looking at her with her pretty hair blowing in the wind."

"Remember that time we stuck gum in her hair?" Mady laughed with watery eyes and a sniffling nose. "It took us hours to get it out. She would refuse to cut her hair. She cried so much that day. Poor Serena, we shouldn't have done that."

I felt quite bad that I didn't have a specific memory of her hair, it was gorgeous and that was about as deep as it got for me. To me, there were many more important qualities. Her mind was a sharp and powerful thing, but she wielded it with love and compassion. God, was she a beautiful person. Her brain held the tabs of every birthday she could remember, and she held tabs on everyone's favorite things. She helped those in need and took nothing in return. She was so kind that it was often people took advantage of her.

"Raven?" Rita breaks through my train of thought.

"Yeah, I remember. What was that scent she always ran through her hair?" I tapped my chin with my finger.

"It used to be vanilla, but the last few months she had changed it to a Rose scent," I said.

"She was warning us..." Mom sighs. "Serena always used to say—"

"Roses smell like death." We all responded.

Five

Rita finished braiding her hair, and she moved on to her face. With a washcloth, she cleaned her eyes, her nose, her cheeks, and every surface available to her. Serena still had a towel rolled up under her chin, keeping her mouth closed. Her face no longer had that rosy hue to it. Her lips were pale and blue. And her eyes were sunken; she looked so tired. How long was she fighting alone? Did she want to tell us? Was she planning to tell us, and time got ahead of her?

It clicked in my head.

"Oh, my God," I said.

"I'll take over, Rita. She loved when I did her makeup. I won't add much. Even in this state, she is the prettiest one of us." Evelyn grabbed a little pink lip balm and gently smudged some on her cheeks. I took out my phone and desperately looked for a voice message from a month ago. Oh God, it couldn't be?

Evelyn brushed her long lashes with a brow comb and kissed each of her eyes. "I'm going to miss those little brown eyes." She sighs and then places lip balm on her mouth, taking her time gliding it on with her finger, when I pressed play.

We all froze at the sound of her voice. I closed my eyes tightly commemorating this to my memory. I wanted to remember her pitch, her timbre, the slight lisp she had when trying to pronounce the letter "S", and the melodic way she tore through our hearts in this partic-ular moment.

"Hey, Raven! I'm hoping to have a talk with everyone soon, I have something...uh...sort of important to tell you all. This Saturday at Mom and Dad's, sounds good? Okay, love you, bye."

I played the message about a dozen times, trying to swal-low the enormous knot in my throat.

"Did we all get that message?" Rita rushed to her phone.
"We blew her off. We always did that. She always wanted to hang out with us, and we kept leaving her on read."

Mady crossed her arms; her cheeks burned red. "Was she there?" She asked Mom.

"She was. Serena said you were all coming, she brought food and board games. I thought you all had planned a game night like the ones you used to have. She never told us she wanted to talk to us about something serious, but she did make sure we would be home."

"We are so fucking blind," I say.

"Why couldn't I have listened?" A sob breaks free from me.

"Why couldn't we all have listened?" They all say.

Six

Serena had a white sheet keeping her covered. The nurses had already removed the previous hospital gown for us. Mady took over now. There was no embarrassment in seeing our sister in such nudity, but it brought back memories of when she was a kid and ran around in only diapers. She was the youngest of us, and we all could relate to that memory. She was a rowdy little thing, unable to sit still at any point in time. It was so unlike her to lie so still; even in her sleep, she would toss and turn and end up in the oddest positions.

As Mady washed her, we all studied our sister. Right now, she has a petite frame and is slim overall. How did we not notice how skinny she got?

Mady used her washcloth to wash her neck, her chest, her breasts, and when she grazed over her poking ribs, we couldn't help but shiver. She was so thin, the stupid disease was eating her inside and out. Her abdomen slightly sank in and put her rib cage on display. We could literally count most of them.

"She had lost her appetite," I said, vividly remembering the last month. "We had gone to eat, and she didn't want to order, so I forced her to. She then barely touched her food and insisted she would eat it at home. I went to visit her the day after and found the food in the garbage. I thought she didn't like the food and was trying not to hurt my feelings since I invited her there." I place my hand on her cold, flat stomach.

"I should have known something was wrong. How did I not notice how thin she had gotten?"

"Look! I didn't know she had a tattoo?" Mady was peeling off some stickers the medical staff left on her chest from the cardiac monitor, and underneath the one that was placed right at the center of her chest was a small set of letters written in cursive.

"REMRS"

"Our initials." Rita grazes the letters with her finger.

"We knew so little about you, my sweet girl." Mom bent herself over and planted a few pecked kisses on Serena's temple.

Serena had the rare ability to make us all feel like shit because she was always such a good person. We used to fight about it, actually. We used to blame her for showing off her altruism, but we were wrong; we were simply trying to find an excuse to feel better about our shitty personalities. In conjunction to her mind, her heart was equally beautiful.

"Do you guys remember when she was terribly sick one day, and she rode the subway, literally on her way to the hospital, because she refused to take an ambulance, convinced that our parents couldn't afford something like that. She didn't want to be a burden. She gave up her seat to an older man with a cane, and she held on to the standing pole, holding on for dear life." Evelyn looked at Serena's chest, as if she could still see her noble heart beating.

"I do remember, what was she thinking?" Mady laughs.

"Of others—" I answer her question. "She always thought of others before herself."

"The person receiving her heart should be warned of the great burden they will carry." Mom said.

"Burden? Serena wasn't a burden?" Rita bites back, offended by the comment.

"Being a good person with a good heart is a burden in the world we live in, honey." Mom said as a matter of fact. With that tone, we knew there was no arguing with her. Besides, we knew she was right. It was way easier to be a mediocre person than one who acted with good intentions, one who followed the moral compass set by the good in her heart.

A heavy burden, that is what Serena's heart will be.

Seven

It's my turn and Mom's again. I take a warm washcloth and begin washing her left arm, and Mom does the same to her right. I can't help but admire her pretty hands. She was an artist; everything she touched was made better or prettier. She inherited that quality from Mom.

I was academically inclined, Mady had a thing going on with sports, Evelyn apparently was part of a band, and Rita was preoccupied playing video games to focus on anything. But Serena was multi-faceted and good at everything. She played a sport, and she excelled. She painted, and it was beautiful. She sang, and the angels sang along with her. She loved, and the world felt her warmth right away.

"Let's paint her nails!" Rita runs to her purse and pulls out bright pink polish.

"You know we aren't supposed to do that, right?" I remind them.

"We weren't supposed to add blush or lip balm either, and here we are." Evelyn rolled her eyes.

"I'm sure it won't hurt, honey. They understand." Mom said.

With that, we took turns painting each finger and decided we would paint her toes only after we washed them.

Her hands already felt cold to the touch, and as much as I squeezed them, hoping she would wake and squeeze mine back. Helplessly hoping that she would wake up and say it was all a prank. But it's not, this is the last moment we get with her, the last girls' night we'll ever have with everyone present. From this day after we will always have a spot empty, we will always be missing someone, and we will always have hope that someday we will meet again in some faraway garden where God keeps his prettiest flowers. I hope he will allow a skeptic like me to at least visit my sister once in a while.

"Aw! They look so pretty, pink is so her color." Rita jumps up and down.

"We all know she preferred green," Evelyn says.

"Nuh uh! Green was her favorite color to look at. Black was her favorite color to wear. But, pink was her current hyper fixation color; her freaking work bag, water bottle, and work shoes were pink." Rita rebuttals.

"We still haven't decided what she should wear...well, you know." Mady stutters.

"To her grave?" Mom clarifies with a sunken nature to her eyes.

It was hard to tell when Mom would break; she is so resilient, but I know that she is breaking for Serena inside. She is so strong; she keeps her heart together with tape that is slowly peeling off, keeping a strong front for us. I just hope she'll be okay. I know Dad is struggling too; he is more upfront about his suffering, though.

The nail polish is drying, and I can't help but weave my finger through hers and plant little kisses on the back of her hand. It was like kissing cold ice, only half expecting the princess of the household to awaken with the kiss of true sisterly love. If that were the case, she would have woken up a long time ago.

Eight

Mady and Rita take over her legs. We used the white sheet to keep her top half and private area covered. They grab the washcloths and start scrubbing at her legs. Her legs were strong. In high school, she was an athlete; she participated in so many sports and in most she over-excelled. Mady and her ended up playing together in many sports teams. I'm sure they had many memories together from meets and matches. Serena eventually got over the athletic scene; she constantly changed her extracurricular activities and ended up doing all kinds of things.

Later in her life, with those legs, she was always a hard worker and she kept on her feet while working long hours. With those same legs, at some point, she also walked herself to a clinic where she was told her life was coming to an end. It's impossible to know when that was. Or why she thought going alone was her best bet.

Rita cleans her feet and takes out the pink polish. Mom helps her paint Serena's toenails. Mom takes her time commending to memory all the fine lines and the shape of her foot.

"I used to grab your little feet when you all were babies and smelled them."

"Gross," Evelyn remarked.

"Not gross at all, you all were my babies, and your feet at the time were cute and not stinky. Your feet, now, however, are questionable. I will likely never willingly smell them again, except..." Mom looked at the freshly cleaned foot of our diseased sister. Without an ounce of remorse, she grabbed her foot and placed a kiss on the top part of each foot.

"My babies will never be gross to me." She said.

"Do you guys remember when she stubbed her toe so hard she fell into the pool. We all laughed and thought she was being dramatic, that we forgot she couldn't swim." Mady said she had stepped back and allowed Mom to have this moment. We all wanted to help, but we could sense that Mom really wanted to do this. She wanted to bathe her baby one last time.

"Yeah, I remember that, thankfully Uncle Murphy realized and jumped in to save her. She could have drowned." I said.

I moved to her feet and placed my hand on top of it, careful not to disturb the fresh polish. The bright pink made an extreme contrast with her rapidly mottling legs and the stark hue of blue on her toes. Even I could acknowledge how fast her body was settling into its new form. We had to hurry.

I look at the clock and notice only thirty minutes have gone by.

Nine

We turn her over to wipe her back. Mady, Rita, and I hold her on her side while Mom and Evelyn wash her back. Evelyn starts with the back of her neck and shoulders. Mom simply adores the lines and muscles that decorate Serena's back. Her back was surprisingly muscular, not bulky at all, but you could tell she was a hard worker. She held so much weight on her back and shoulders, whether that was the weight of her stresses, or work, or her rapidly consuming illness.

Serena was one to bottle up feelings and deal with her own burdens silently because she didn't want to burden anyone. We always had to force the truth out of her. I wonder why we didn't do that this time? We didn't even notice that something was wrong in the first place. How blind could we have been? She worked hard even in her last days. Even while thin, we could still see how much effort she put into her last days through the striations of the muscles in her back.

"Just yesterday, she had asked me if I could give her a shoulder rub. I said no." Evelyn said with the ghost of yesterdays past nagging at her. "I should have said yes." Her hands gently rubbed the back of her shoulders.

"I remember when she had a back injury at her job," I said. "She would constantly ask us for massages, but never complained about being in pain. We couldn't have known something was wrong."

"Serena simply didn't want us to know, honey." Mom bent forward and placed a small kiss between her shoulder blades.

Ten

Mom took over cleaning her bottom and private area. We stood on the opposite side holding her on her right side. Rita swapped places with me, and I helped clean the back of Serena's legs. Mom cleaned her with a practiced motion as if she were doing this all her life. I looked at the number of girls she had birthed and confirmed my suspicion. She definitely had wiped countless butts, specifically all of the butts in this room.

"Serena would always cry when I changed her diaper when she was a baby. For the most part, the rest of you would keep playing and didn't mind the change at all. She hated it when I changed her diaper. She would kick and roll trying to get away and ended up making a bigger mess for me to clean up." A small smile tugged at Mom's cheek, as if the memory warmed her soul while cleaning her daughter again.

I'm sure we all never thought the day would come when we witnessed Mom wiping one of us as if we were babies. Well, we are all still her babies. Mom did a thorough job and was tempted to grab diaper rash cream, but I reminded her that we had broken too many rules regarding her bath already.

This was it, the last part of this commemoration had come. We gently laid her on her back and made sure to straighten her out. Making sure she looked comfortable.

If I squinted, the signs of death disappeared, and she only looked as if she were sleeping. Who knew an hour would feel like five minutes? We took a fresh white sheet and covered her up to her shoulders. We took turns whispering into her ear. Our thanks, regrets, and goodbyes. I was second to last, and I was losing my grip on myself. How could I say goodbye to her? She was like my baby. As the eldest, I took care of her while Mom and Dad were at work. I watched all of them grow. I watched all of them cry and get sick. I was strict at times, and we got on each other's nerves. We are sisters after all.

I close the distance between us, kneel at her side, and let my heart speak for me. Except the words wouldn't come out. I choked on the knot in my throat; I couldn't, and yet I forced myself.

"Baby Serena, oh how I wish so many things had played out differently," I sobbed, "How I wish I could have noticed you were struggling, or that you had changed so much in a span of months. How I wish I could have listened to you and all of your dying wishes. But at least we all got to hold your hand while you were laid to rest. I'm sorry I didn't tell you how much I love you when you could still hear me. I'm sorry I didn't get to say I love you enough. Everything happened so suddenly and so fast. None of us saw it coming. Oh, my baby sis!"

This was what regret and heartbreak felt like. "We still had so many pending conversations, jokes, and special moments in our lives. How fleeting is time, but death is unprecedented and we forget that we must cherish each other as time is never guaranteed. I love you tons, and I hope there is an afterlife where I get to at least visit you once or twice. I already miss you, and I can't imagine what the rest of my life will be without you." With that, I plant a kiss on her temple and take a good, hard look at her. This isn't how I wanted to remember her, but this is the moment when I realized she did, in fact, smell of Roses, even when the room was covered in Tulips.

"Turns out you were right, Serena, Roses do smell like death."

Mom followed, and we couldn't muster to keep our tears contained as we saw a Mother saying her final goodbye to her child. In a gut-wrenching moment, Mom still did not let any tears spill. I'm not sure how she managed not to, but her eyes did not lie. There was a dullness to them that I had never seen in her. She held her baby in her hands, and I could tell she didn't want to leave her. But time was of the essence, and someone else might be waiting to receive the gift of life through my sister. She had made that decision for us.

Eleven

The nurses entered the room, grabbed the bed by the sides, and drove the bed out of the room. They instructed us to follow close behind. But before that, they ushered Dad back into the room, and he also had another moment to fall apart in Serena's arms. He was not able to contain himself; unlike Mom, he showed his emotions so openly, and goodbyes were the hardest for him.

The remaining family in the waiting room was also directed and ushered to the hallway, where the Honor walk would take place. The seventh floor, apparently, was the closest to the surgical room where Serena's organs would be harvested. Considering she had stage four cancer, I'm not sure what organs they could even harvest; that whole process was very confusing to us still.

We followed close behind her bed as we entered the elevator. Mom held Dad tightly, and we held each other. God, was the elevator ride long, I wanted to climb into bed and cuddle with my sister as we used to do when we were kids. I wanted to tell her bedtime stories and lull her to sleep. I wanted to taunt her and tell her the monster under the bed would get her. Except in this nightmare, the monster with the big C did in fact get her, and that monster was cruel and would never return her.

We arrived on the seventh floor, and we exited the elevator. Mom and Dad stood at either side of the bed, and they both held one of Serena's hands. As we descended down a very long hallway, towards a mysterious entrance. We walked behind the nurse and watched as we slowly passed our family, workers, and other bystanders paying respect to my sister.

They paid respect to what she was about to do. But we paid respect to her memory and the loss of a beautiful soul. Dad cried as his head hung forward, and Mom wore a zombie-like expression. I think her brain numbed her so much from the immense pain that she was no longer able to cry at all. The closer we got to the door, the scarier the hallway was. This has to be a nightmare, right? I have to wake up. There is no way Serena is dead. The hallway slowly became eerie, black and white with flickering strobing lights. Cobwebs strung from the ceiling and the door at the end transformed into a black hole, trying to eat Serena's sleeping body alive.

"No. Get it together." I thought.

I blinked, and the hallway was back to normal, and we had arrived at the door. My parents were forced to let go of her hands, and we were no longer allowed to go with her. One final kiss from each of us. And we watched them walk through the door, to do God knows what. As if in slow motion, the door closed, and that was that. The next time we get to see her would be at her funeral.

Twelve

A week went by, during which we went through her stuff and had endless arguments about what Serena's resting outfit would be. We fought more than usual that week, and Mom was still eerily calm. Deep purple eye bags haunted her face, and her cheekbones started to sink from her lack of appetite. Mom stood aside and let us sift through Serena's belongings for a while.

We read through Serena's journals and sifted through her books until Mom kicked us out of her room and started sleeping there instead. She refused to wash her clothes and covers. Her scent was still in them, and goodness would she try to prolong Serena's presence in the house.

Aside from that, she left her room as it was, refusing to believe that one of her babies was truly gone. What pain it must be to watch a child die, when you are supposed to die before them. What a reminder of life's cruel nature. What a reminder that time is not promised.

We arrived at the mortuary early and gave them the outfit we wanted her to wear. We settled for a flowy white dress and no shoes. We asked that her hair be kept wild with her natural wave pattern and that her makeup look as natural as possible. We gave them tons of flowers to place inside her casket, just as she had mentioned a few years ago when we had a random conversation about what we wanted at our funerals. Who knew that information would become handy so soon?

"I want a simple casket, preferably of wood. And, I want to be surrounded by flowers. Tulips, Angel's Breath, and only in that case will I accept roses, but make sure they are yellow." Serena had said.

And we did exactly that. We selected a simple wooden casket with a very light wood stain color. I knew she was dead, yet it still felt unnatural to choose her casket. As if this was still happening. But it was, wasn't it? I still had hope that I would wake up from this terrible nightmare.

The time for her funeral arrived, and we ensured everything was perfect. There were snacks and coffee, and lots of areas to sit to watch the vigil until tomorrow morning, when we will caravan to the cemetery.

The funeral home was full to the brim. So many people came to pay their respects, so many people cried over her death. I had not realized how much of an imprint she left behind. I didn't realize how many people truly cared about her. I shouldn't be surprised; she was the kindest person I knew by far.

There was not a single point during the night when there was less than fifty people in the funeral home. It was slightly alarming, actually. Close family, distant family flew in. Close friends and old classmates. Her coworkers from multiple places of work attended. My Parent's friends and coworkers, some of my friends, and my siblings friends. So many people came to see her rest.

She did look beautiful in her casket. Dad had yelled at me for saying that out loud. But I don't think I said anything wrong. Being dead does not mean she is any less beautiful. She looked perfectly serene in the center of her casket. She was surrounded by flowers neatly tucked underneath her and sprouting around her, an aura of florals, and in the center, she lies, with wild hair framing her beautiful face. They did an amazing job with her makeup; she did not look dead at all.

The whole night, I had a tinge of hope that she would once again sit up and announce a prank. God, how much I wanted to go shake her shoulders and yell at her for making us worry like this. How dare she play this prank on us! This whole thing was so cruel! I could never forgive her for hurting our family like this.

"She can't be gone—" I thought.

But how could I not forgive such a heavenly woman? How could I not love her so much? This was reality, and oh, how cruel she was. This was not her fault at all, but I just needed something to blame; it was easy to blame her for the pain her absence caused in me. My thought process was interrupted by a small chime from the televisions that were playing all kinds of slide shows with pictures of her and our family, highlighting all of the important moments of her life.

A video started playing, and that video was the death of me.

It started with baby Serena, crying in Mom's arms a day or two after she was born, and Dad looked so unbelievably happy. That was the thing about our Parent's, they really wanted to be parents. Then the video transitions to toddler Serena, and she was wearing her little princess costume, prancing around while singing the tune of her favorite princess. She looked so goofy, I remembered that moment actually. We would tell her to shut up all of the time because she wouldn't stop singing it. Now, we see teenage Serena, her most annoying version yet. The video was of all of us sitting around in the living room having a game night. She was crying because she was always a sore loser. Then lastly, it was her graduation video. Mom had the bright idea to do a mock interview so she could see it years from that moment, or to show her future kids. This was only two years ago.

"Serena, tell us how it feels to graduate from college?" Mom asked behind the camera.

"Well, it's a great blessing. I am really excited to start my professional life." She had said, looking awkwardly at the side of the camera. Evelyn and Rita were there trying to make her laugh and mess up her mock interview.

"Is there something that you would like to tell your future self?" Mom asked, and then shushed my sisters.

"Future Serena, I'm proud of you, and I love you! Cherish every moment you have, work hard, and never forget to say I love you. I hope you're happy." She was looking straight at the camera, and for an instant it felt as if she were talking to all of us. My heart collapsed and fell so hard it slammed straight into my stomach.

"Okay, Serena. Say bye to the camera." Mom had said in the video.

"Bye-bye! Love you!" She waved and blew a kiss, and with that, the video ended.

Thirteen

We rode behind the hearse in Dad's truck; that video was a punch in the gut. We haven't been able to muster a single word.

Dad's eyes are swollen still. He was able to thank all of our guests, and he was the first into the car. Through the window, you could see how much he was crying. I have never seen someone cry this much before. I cried as well. I was not as strong as Mom. Throughout the vigil, my sisters and I took turns holding each other. Sitting next to Dad, and watching Mom intently, worried that she would break soon, and we wanted to make sure we were there for her.

The car ride was quite long, and we had police officers escorting us. No one in the family was expecting such a sudden tragedy. Serena could steal hearts and spread happiness; it was rare when someone did not like her or fell in love with her. Although she was not perfect, and

I am sure she had made her own handful of mistakes, to me, none of those will ever be worth mentioning. She is my sister, and even in death, I will love her forever.

We arrived at her burial site, but her headstone had not arrived yet. We also chose a very simple one as she had requested.

My parents brought a priest, and he blessed her body. She was lowered six feet under, and we made it rain flower petals on top of her casket before covering it up with dirt. Dad sang with the mariachi band, as he let his soul be consoled by the music.

Some time went by, and everyone accompanying us started to leave. Only when we were all alone: Dad, Mom, Mady, Rita, Evelyn, Me and Serena, did Mom get on her knees and take out a few seeds from her pocket. She planted them in the center of her burial site, patted them down, and poured some water on top. We all watched as she planted the flower seeds and finished up by sticking a single Tulip in the dirt.

"She truly was the most beautiful flower."

And Mom finally cried.

About the Author

Hello, P.R. Miguel here. First and foremost I want to thank everyone who has taken the time to read any of my writing. I know I tend to gravitate towards grim topic as I aspire to open conversation of difficult topics through narratives. This short story was inspired by some encounters I've had with death through my years in healthcare. I see how different people cope and I wanted to highlight that through the different ways some of the characters were processing the event in the story.

As some of you may know, this is the second book I publish, and although it is a short story I do hold it near and dear to my heart, as this story is a reality we all confront at some point in our lives. I am very proud to keep growing as an author, and sometimes in writing less is more and that is what I think this short story is.

Thank you again and I hope to continue fostering your support.

Sincerely, your new favorite author.

Rogue Reaper: A Fight for Life in Death by P.R. Miguel

Also By:

This is an adult Fiction-Fantasy book following psycho-logical and ethical themes, as well as action, battles, fun banter, and a subplot of romance.

Opal Tempest awakens in the afterlife only to find out her judgment is nullified because she committed suicide. The Gods sentenced her to one hundred Earth years of

Reaper service and an eternity in the Underworld after. The law of the Reaper is that they don't interfere with death, but simply escort souls to judgment. Upon the start of her sentence, she discovers a truth that shakes her moral compass. An external force, known as Rogues, plagues humans, coercing them to commit suicide. With this information, she realizes that suicide is not completely autonomous and believes the system is not fair. Through her service collecting souls, she confronts a situation that forces her to make a decision: complete her sentence and ignore her moral compass, or break the rules and upset the balance of the afterlife. Which will she choose?

The story follows an ethical debate regarding justice, mental health, and suicide, with a character who fights for life in death, and a set of Gods considering that their law is not perfect. Follow Opal through her journey of self-reflection, forgiveness, and the realization that there is more to death than she thought.

www.ingramcontent.com/pod-product-compliance
Lightning Source LLC
Chambersburg PA
CBHW012028110726
47995CB00006B/1171